ASTRID & APOLLO

C

IN CONCERT

BY
V.T. BIDANIA

ILLUSTRATED BY
EVELT YANAIT

PICTURE WINDOW BOOKS
a capstone imprint

To Trystan —VTB

Published by Picture Window Books,
an imprint of Capstone.
1710 Roe Crest Drive
North Mankato, Minnesota 56003
capstonepub.com

Text copyright © 2021 by V.T. Bidania.
Illustrations copyright © 2021 by Capstone.

Library of Congress Cataloging-in-Publication Data
Names: Bidania, V.T., author. | Yanait, Evelt, illustrator.
Title: Astrid and Apollo in concert / by V.T. Bidania ; illustrated by Evelt Yanait.
Description: North Mankato, Minnesota : Picture Window Books, [2021] |
Series: Astrid and Apollo | Audience: Ages 6-8. | Audience: Grades K-1.|
Summary: As Astrid and Apollo practice for their duet in the recorder concert they become increasingly frustrated with their little sister Eliana, who keeps getting in the way, but when events leading up to the concert do not go as planned the twins realize just how much Eliana feels left out. Includes facts about the Hmong.
Identifiers: LCCN 2021002510 (print) | LCCN 2021002511 (ebook) |
ISBN 9781663908711 (hardcover) | ISBN 9781663920171 (paperback) |
ISBN 9781663908681 (ebook pdf)
Subjects: CYAC: Twins—Fiction. | Brothers and sisters—Fiction. |
Concerts—Fiction. | Hmong Americans—Fiction.
Classification: LCC PZ7.1.B5333 Av 2021 (print) | LCC PZ7.1.B5333 (ebook) | DDC [E]—dc23
LC record available at https://lccn.loc.gov/2021002510
LC ebook record available at https://lccn.loc.gov/2021002511

Designer: Kay Fraser

Design Elements: Capstone/Dara Lashia Lee, 61; Shutterstock: Ingo Menhard, 60, Yangxiong (pattern), 5 and throughout

Printed and bound in the USA. 4270

Table of Contents

Hi, I'm Astrid. My twin brother is Apollo, and we were born in Minnesota. We live here with our mom, dad, and little sister, Eliana.

ASTRID GAO NOU

Hi, I'm Apollo! Our mom and dad were both born in Laos. They came to the United States when they were very young and grew up here.

APOLLO NOU KOU

MOM, DAD, AND ELIANA GAO CHEE

HMONG WORDS

gao (GOW)—girl; it is often placed in front of a girl's name. Hmong spelling: *nkauj*

Gao Chee (GOW chee)—shiny girl. Hmong spelling: *Nkauj Ci*

Gao Hlee (GOW lee)—moon girl. Hmong spelling: *Nkauj Hlis*

Gao Nou (GOW new)—sun girl. Hmong spelling: *Nkauj Hnub*

Hmong (MONG)—a group of people who came to the U.S. from Laos. Many Hmong from Laos now live in Minnesota. Hmong spelling: *Hmoob*

Nou Kou (NEW koo)—star. Hmong spelling: *Hnub Qub*

pa dow (PA dah-oh)—needlework made of shapes like flowers, triangles, and swirls. Hmong spelling: *paj ntaub*

pho gao (fuh gow)—steamed rice rolls made from rice flour and water and filled with ground meat, onions, and other seasonings. Hmong spelling: *fawm kauv*

tou (TOO)—boy or son; it is often placed in front of a boy's name. Hmong spelling: *tub*

CHAPTER 1

Duet

Astrid and Apollo stepped off the school bus. They ran down the block to their house.

"I'm so excited!" said Astrid.

"Wait until we tell them!" said Apollo.

They went up the steps to the front door and hurried inside.

"Mom!" Astrid called out.

"We're home!" said Apollo.

They dropped their backpacks and took off their shoes. The house smelled good.

Astrid sniffed the air. She smelled onions. She saw bags of white rice flour on the kitchen table. "Is Mom making pho gao?"

"I hope so! Anything with pho in it sounds good to me!" said Apollo.

Luna barked and ran over. Eliana came too.

"Hi!" Eliana said.

"Hi, Eliana!" said Astrid. Then she picked up the puppy.

"Did you have a good day?" Apollo asked his little sister.

Eliana nodded and smiled.

Mom poked her head out of the kitchen. "Hi, kids," she said.

"We have news!" Apollo announced.

Mom walked over. Her apron had pa dow designs on it. She wiped her hands, dusting the apron with flour.

"What is it?" she asked.

Astrid grinned. "Today in music class, Ms. Williams talked about our recorder concert. It's coming up!" She looked at Apollo.

"She told us who gets to play solos . . . ," Apollo said.

"And?" Mom asked.

The twins smiled but didn't say anything.

Mom looked at them curiously. "Tell me!" she begged.

Eliana was curious too. Even Luna seemed to want to know. She wiggled her ears and wagged her tail.

Astrid and Apollo laughed.

Mom laughed too. "Well, what about the solos?"

Apollo pointed at Astrid and at himself. "Ms. Williams picked us to do a solo! Well, it won't be a solo because it's two of us. It'll be a duet. We get to play 'Sparkle, Sparkle Giant Moon'!"

"It'll be just the two of us playing in front of the whole school!" said Astrid.

Mom put her hands over her heart. "That's wonderful!" she exclaimed.

"Mom, Ms. Williams said our notes sound 'just lovely!'" said Apollo.

"Excellent news. I'm so happy for you!" Mom hugged the twins.

Luna jumped from Astrid's arms and landed by Eliana's feet.

Eliana wanted a hug too. She pushed her way between her mother, brother, and sister. She pushed so hard that Astrid bumped into Apollo. Then Apollo bumped into Mom. Then Mom almost tripped on Luna!

"Eliana, careful!" Mom said.

Eliana moved back. She crossed her arms and made a face.

Apollo picked up his backpack. "Come on, Astrid. We'd better start practicing. The concert's only two weeks away."

"You're right. We don't have much time," Astrid agreed.

"I'm making pho gao. I'll let you know when it's ready," Mom said.

"Yes, I knew it!" said Astrid.

"Thanks, Mom! Can you make mine extra spicy?" Apollo asked.

"Of course," Mom said with a smile.

Apollo took his recorder from his backpack. Astrid got her recorder too and followed him to the living room.

Eliana started to follow too, but Mom took her hand.

"Come help me roll the pho gao," Mom said.

Eliana made another face.

CHAPTER 2

Trumpet Man

After dinner, Astrid said, "Apollo and I will play some songs for you tonight."

"How exciting!" said Mom.

"I cannot wait," Dad said.

Apollo carried the music stand and music folder to the living room. Astrid carried their recorders.

They saw Eliana in front of the TV. She was lying on her stomach, holding her chin in her hands. Luna lay next to her.

Eliana was watching a music show. A guitar player and a drummer were on a stage playing a song. A man with a trumpet joined them.

The song had a fast and fun beat. The man blew into the trumpet. He moved from side to side and did a silly dance.

Eliana laughed. Astrid and Apollo laughed too.

Dad walked into the room. "I'm so proud of my twins. They're going to be in concert!" he said.

He sat on the couch and turned off the TV. "Sit with me, Eliana. Let's hear the twins play."

Eliana sat next to Dad. Luna jumped up onto Dad's lap.

Apollo pulled sheets of music from the folder and placed them on the music stand. He said, "We will play 'Cold Round Rolls,' 'Mario Had a Huge Sheep,' and 'The Icky, Biggy Buggy' first."

Dad nodded. Eliana shrugged. Luna rested her head on Dad's knee.

"After that, we will play 'Sparkle, Sparkle Giant Moon' for you," Astrid added.

"Wow! You're playing four songs for the concert?" Dad asked.

"Wait for me!" Mom said. She came in and sat next to Eliana. "I thought you were playing one song?"

"Our class will play three songs together," said Astrid. "Then Apollo and I will play 'Sparkle, Sparkle Giant Moon' for our duet."

"Okay, we're ready!" Mom said.

Astrid and Apollo raised the recorders to their mouths. Astrid said to Apollo, "I'll count. We start after three."

Apollo nodded.

"One, two, three," said Astrid. Then they both started playing.

Mom and Dad smiled. Eliana smiled. Even Luna looked happy as soft music came from the recorders. The notes sounded lovely, just like Ms. Williams said.

Suddenly, Eliana stood up and left the room. Luna hopped off the couch and followed her.

A minute later, Eliana and Luna came back. Eliana was holding a paper party horn. It was from her last birthday party. Eliana put the horn in her mouth and blew. A loud, squeaky sound came out as the blue paper horn unrolled like a lizard's tongue.

Astrid and Apollo stopped playing.

"Hey!" said Astrid.

Eliana blew again, harder this time. Her cheeks puffed out. Luna cocked her head.

"Quit it!" said Apollo.

"Eliana, please stop," said Dad.

But Eliana kept blowing. Luna ran behind the couch.

"She's being like the trumpet man on TV!" said Astrid with a frown.

"Are you the trumpet man?" asked Apollo.

Eliana nodded and danced from side to side, just like the man had done.

Dad reached for Eliana. "It's the twins' turn now. Then you can have a turn."

Eliana shook her head and blew louder.

"Make her stop!" Astrid pleaded.

"Eliana Gao Chee, stop blowing that horn right now," Mom said.

Eliana's face grew red. She threw the horn on the floor and screamed. That was even louder than the horn!

Astrid put her hands on her ears.
Apollo hit his hand on his
forehead and said, "Eliana, be quiet!"
Eliana kept screaming. Luna
started barking.

"That's enough," said Dad. He picked up Eliana and carried her out of the room. She kicked and screamed as loud as she could.

* * * * *

The next day, Astrid and Apollo came home with more news to share.

"Mom, Ms. Williams said we should dress in nice clothes for the concert," said Astrid.

"You have so many pretty outfits. What would you like to wear?" asked Mom.

Astrid thought for a moment. "How about my silver dress with the sparkly skirt? It will go with the 'Sparkle, Sparkle' song!"

"Great idea. What about you, Apollo?" Mom asked.

"Can I wear a shirt and tie? And I need to wear black shoes," he said.

"Sure, you already have a nice shirt and tie. For shoes, what about your dress shoes from the Hmong New Year?" Mom asked.

"Oh yeah!" Apollo opened the front closet and pulled out the shoes. He tried to slip them on his feet, but they were too tight. "Mom, they don't fit anymore!"

Mom picked up one shoe. "Your feet have grown a lot. These won't work," she said.

"But I have to wear black shoes," said Apollo.

Mom said, "We'll go shopping this weekend. We'll get you new shoes."

"Thanks, Mom," said Apollo.

Mom turned to Astrid. "I remember seeing a silver headband at the store. It had a shiny moon and star design on it. It would match your dress perfectly. Would you like to get it?"

"Yes, please!" said Astrid.

CHAPTER 3

Bravo

For the next two weeks, Astrid and Apollo practiced every day after school. Then they practiced again after dinner.

Luna liked to watch them play. She sat on the floor in front of them. Sometimes she fell asleep to the music!

Eliana didn't want to watch. She wanted to play with them. She brought her party horn to the living room when the twins practiced.

But Mom and Dad said Eliana had to wait until Astrid and Apollo were done. So Eliana had to find other things to do to keep busy.

* * * * *

Sunday was the night before the concert. At dinnertime, Astrid said, "We will do one last practice show for you tonight."

"Sounds great!" said Dad as he bit into a spring roll.

"Are you excited for tomorrow?" Mom asked. She put a spring roll on Eliana's plate.

Eliana opened the roll and spread it out. She picked out the vegetables and stuffed the rice noodles and meat into her mouth.

Apollo dipped his roll into the spicy peanut sauce. "I'm nervous," he admitted.

"So am I. But excited at the same time," Astrid said with a grin.

"Well, you've been working very hard. You practice two times a day—every day! I think you'll both do great at the concert," Dad said.

"I agree!" said Mom.

"Thanks!" Astrid and Apollo said together.

"See, you're good at duets!" Dad said with a laugh.

* * * * *

After dinner, Apollo put on his new black shoes. Astrid wore her new sparkly headband. They set up their sheet music on the stand and took out their recorders.

"You both look amazing!" Mom said.

"Yes, you're very fancy tonight," said Dad. "I like the new shoes, Apollo. And that's the shiniest hair head thing I've ever seen, Astrid."

Astrid laughed. "It's called a headband!"

"It's the shiniest headband," Dad corrected himself.

"Would you like to sit with us, Eliana?" Mom asked.

Eliana was sitting at the coffee table coloring. She had glue, scissors, crayons, and paper spread out.

She took a drink from her cup of milk and said, "Nope way."

Mom shrugged. "Go ahead and begin," she said to the twins.

Astrid and Apollo lifted their recorders to their mouths. Astrid counted to three, and they played their songs.

When they were done, Dad clapped and said, "Bravo!"

"You sounded fabulous!" Mom clapped with him. "That practice has really paid off."

Astrid and Apollo smiled and bowed.

Mom stood up. "This calls for bubble tea! I picked up your favorite flavors today. Coconut for Astrid. Vanilla for Apollo. And strawberry for Eliana," she said.

"I'll help," Dad offered.

After Mom and Dad left for the kitchen, the twins decided to practice their duet song one more time.

"We need to be sure we really know it," said Apollo.

"At least we don't have to memorize it," said Astrid.

She opened the folder and took out the music for "Sparkle, Sparkle, Giant Moon." She put the other music on the coffee table.

Astrid and Apollo began to play. Eliana looked at the music. She looked at Astrid and Apollo. Then she picked up a piece of paper and a crayon. As Astrid and Apollo played, Eliana began to draw.

The duet was nearly finished when Eliana ran up to the music stand. She pushed the twins' sheet music off and put the drawing she had made on the stand instead.

"Hey, what are you doing?" asked Apollo.

Eliana pointed to her drawing.

"See!" she said.

"We are trying to practice," Astrid explained.

"See!" Eliana said again.

"Eliana," Apollo said with a sigh. He picked up the sheet music off the floor and put it back on the stand. He gave the drawing back to Eliana.

"Pway!" Eliana said. She tried to give him the drawing again.

"We can't play that!" said Astrid.

"Pway, pway, pway!" Eliana screamed.

"Stop screaming, Eliana!" Apollo said.

Eliana frowned. She made fists at her sides. Then she ran to the bathroom and slammed the door.

Mom and Dad walked into the room with cups of bubble tea.

"What happened?" asked Mom.

"Let me guess. Eliana?" said Dad.

Astrid and Apollo nodded.

CHAPTER 4

Don't Worry

The night of the concert had arrived.

Eliana was playing with Luna on the carpet. She threw a toy ball across the room.

"Luna Luna, ball!" Eliana said.

Luna ran to the other side of the room. She sniffed the ball. Then she came back and sat next to Eliana, without the ball.

"Ball!" Eliana said.

Luna put her paws out in front of her. She leaned her body forward. But she wouldn't go after the ball.

"No ball." Eliana sighed and shook her head.

"Eliana, please put Luna in her kennel. We're leaving soon," said Mom.

"Luna Luna, kennel up!" said Eliana.

Mom stood at the bottom of the stairs and said, "Astrid and Apollo, are you ready? It's almost time to go."

Apollo came down the steps. He was wearing a shirt with a blue tie and black pants. "I just have to put on my shoes," he said and walked to the front closet.

All of a sudden, Astrid let out a loud shriek from upstairs.

Right at that moment, Apollo yelled too.

Eliana disappeared down the hall.

"What happened?" Mom asked. She hurried up the stairs. "I'll check on her. You check on him!" she said to Dad.

Dad rushed over to the closet.

Apollo was holding one shoe. "There's milk in my shoes! My socks are all wet!"

Milk dripped from his shoe. A white puddle was spreading across the floor.

"How did that happen? Bring it to the sink!" said Dad.

At the sink, Apollo poured out the milk. "I can't wear these!"

"Don't worry. We'll rinse them out," said Dad. He turned on the water. Water and milk splashed all over.

"It's all wet! What am I going to do?" said Apollo.

Mom and Astrid came down the stairs.

Astrid was wearing her silver dress, but her hair was a mess. The sparkly headband hung from her hair in a tangle. Her face was red.

"I can't believe it!" Astrid said.

"You'll be okay," said Mom.

Mom told Astrid to sit on a chair. She tried to pull the headband off, but it was stuck.

Astrid's hair was covered in glue!

"We might have to cut it off," Mom said. She pulled at the glue in Astrid's hair.

"What? I can't get a haircut now! What am I going to do?" Astrid started to cry.

"Don't worry. We'll fix this," Mom said.

Astrid frowned. "It was Eliana. She put glue on my headband!"

Apollo came into the living room. "And she poured milk in my shoes!"

"I'm so mad at her!" said Astrid.

"Me too!" said Apollo.

"Calm down, everyone," Dad said. "Apollo, maybe we can we put your shoes in the dryer. Astrid, can we wash the glue out of your hair?"

"We need to be at the school soon," Mom reminded them.

"My shoes will still smell like rotten milk!" Apollo whined.

"And my hair will still be sticky!" Astrid moaned.

"Okay, we'll have to think of something else, fast," said Dad.

Mom went to the closet and came back with a hat and a different pair of shoes.

"There's no more time! This will have to do. Kids, get in the car," she said.

"Aren't you forgetting someone?" Dad asked.

"I'll get Eliana," Mom said.

CHAPTER 5

Bow

Mom, Dad, and Eliana found seats in the second row. The school auditorium was crowded, but a nice family moved their jackets and gave them two seats. Dad sat in one. Eliana sat on Mom's lap in the other.

They watched as the third-grade class played their songs. Everyone clapped.

Then it was time for Astrid and Apollo's duet.

They walked to the center of the stage while Ms. Williams spoke to the audience. They put their folder on the music stand.

Astrid had a pink beret on her head. It covered almost all of her hair. Apollo wore his black winter boots.

Astrid looked at the audience. She could see Eliana's face in the second row.

Eliana looked sad. No one had said a word on the drive to the concert.

"I feel bad," Astrid whispered to Apollo.

Apollo saw Eliana too. She was watching them with big eyes.

"So do I," Apollo said. "Maybe we could have been nicer to her. She felt left out."

Ms. Williams thanked the parents and families for coming to the concert. She talked about music and about their unit on recorders.

As Ms. Williams talked, Astrid opened the folder. She saw the other three songs they had just played. But she needed the music for "Sparkle, Sparkle, Giant Moon." She pulled out the last sheet in the back of the folder and put it on the stand.

Then her eyes opened wide. Astrid turned to look at Apollo.

He was staring at the paper.

"Oh no!" whispered Astrid.

The sheet wasn't the music for
their song. It was Eliana's drawing.

She had used a black crayon to
make rows across the paper. Over
the rows were big dots in different
colors. The dots had short lines and
little flags. Eliana had drawn her
own musical notes.

Astrid flipped through the other sheets again, trying to find their duet piece. But it was gone.

"What are we going to do?" Astrid's hands started to shake. Her stomach felt like it was doing flips.

Apollo blinked and swallowed hard. "It's too late! We just have to play it from memory," he whispered.

"Memory?" said Astrid.

Apollo nodded. "I know you can do it. We practiced so much."

Astrid took a deep breath.

"Thanks, Apollo. I know you can do it too," she said.

Then Ms. Williams was done talking. She nodded at Astrid and Apollo.

The audience clapped. The lights dimmed. A spotlight fell straight onto the twins. Everyone watched and waited.

Astrid looked at Apollo. She slowly mouthed *one, two, three.* Then she and Apollo began to play.

Their fingers moved over the finger holes. They blew carefully into the mouthpieces. They played the beginning of the song, just like they had practiced.

The music flowed from the recorders. Then they got to the middle of the song. Their hearts were beating so fast.

Apollo took a quick breath and when he blew, he made a squeak.

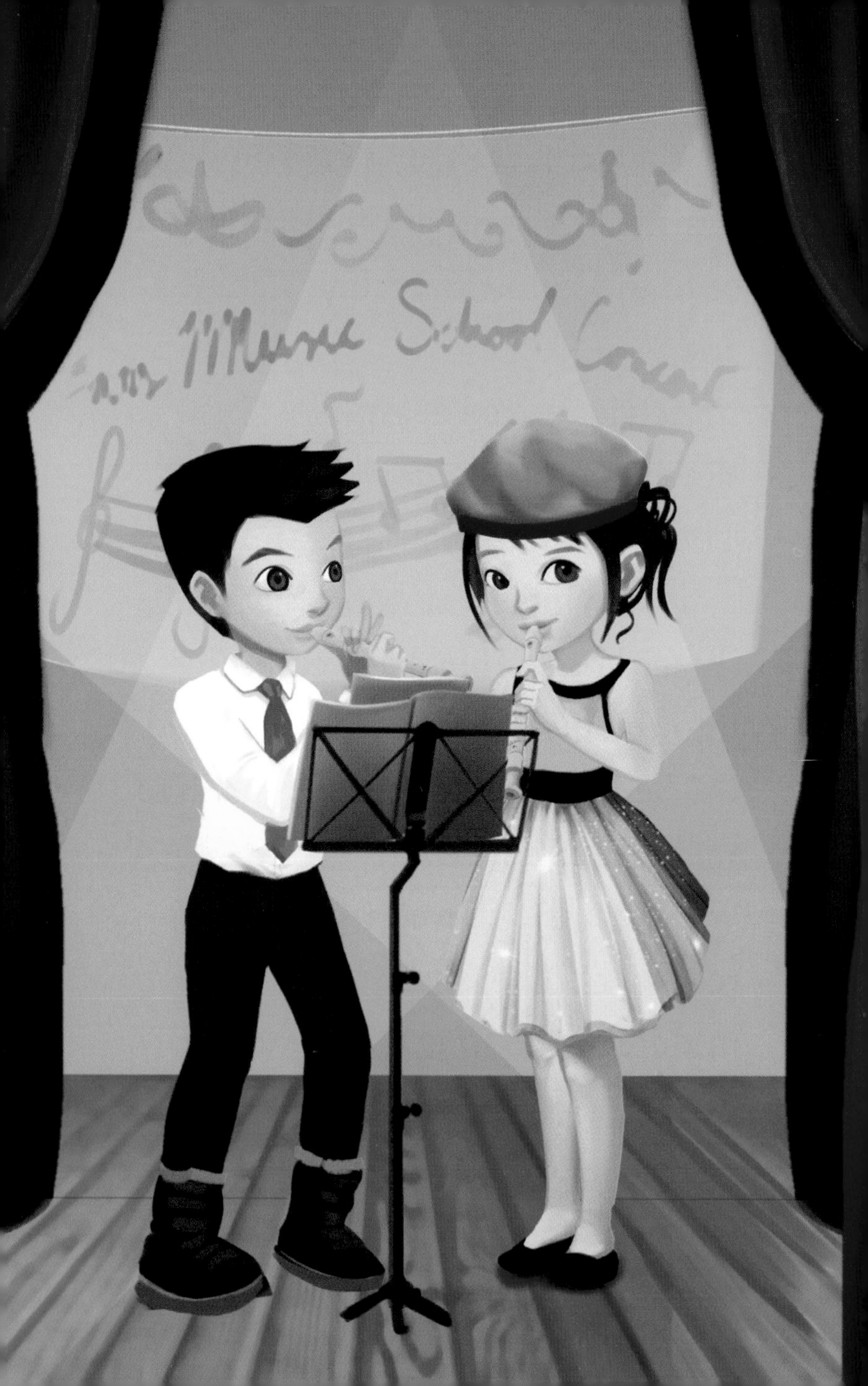
Music School

Astrid heard the squeak and started playing too fast. But Apollo kept playing, and Astrid slowed down. Soon they were in step again. The notes sounded lovely.

Then they got to the end of the song and finished the last note together.

The audience clapped loudly. The light from Dad's camera flashed as he took pictures. People even cheered.

Astrid and Apollo looked out at the audience. They looked at each other. They saw Ms. Williams on the side of the stage. She smiled and whispered, "Bow."

The twins leaned forward and bowed.

* * * *

Astrid and Apollo waited for Mom and Dad at the side of the stage. When they saw them in the crowd, they made their way down the stage steps.

"Mom! Dad!" they called. Astrid and Apollo hurried over and went straight to Eliana.

Apollo picked her up, and they both gave their little sister a big hug.

"We're sorry, Eliana," Apollo said.

Mom and Dad looked at them, confused.

"We should have let you practice with us, Eliana Gao Chee," Astrid said.

Eliana nodded.

"We didn't mean to make you feel left out. We're sorry, okay? And thank you for your music," said Apollo.

He set Eliana down. Then he pulled her drawing from the music folder to show Mom and Dad.

"She made this for us. Look at the back," Apollo said.

Dad looked at the drawing and turned it over. He smiled. Then he showed it to Mom.

She smiled too.

On one side were musical notes in different colors. On the back, Eliana had drawn a picture of the three of them. Astrid and Apollo were playing their recorders. Eliana was playing her party horn. She had drawn a wobbly heart around all three of them.

"Beautiful, Eliana," Mom said. She gave Eliana a hug.

Then she said to Astrid and Apollo, "You both did a wonderful job tonight."

"We're so proud of you," said Dad.

Mom held up the drawing again.

"And it was very nice of you to apologize to your sister," she said. "We had a talk with Eliana."

"Eliana, is there something you want to say to your brother and sister?" Dad asked.

Eliana nodded. "Sowwy for the milk. Sowwy for the goo," she said.

Then Eliana pointed at her drawing, which she had switched with their music. "Sowwy 'bout that."

Astrid and Apollo laughed. "It's okay."

Then Eliana looked at their recorders and said, "Now we pway together?"

She reached into her pocket and pulled out her party horn.

Just as she put it to her mouth, Dad threw his hand out. "Let's just wait until we get to the car, okay?"

In the car, Mom and Dad laughed and covered their ears and opened the windows. Astrid and Apollo played their recorders, and Eliana blew her party horn all the way home.

- Hmong people first lived in southern China. Many of them moved to Southeast Asia in the 1800s. Some Hmong decided to stay in the country of Laos (pronounced *LAH-ohs*).

LAOS

- In the 1950s, a war called the Vietnam War started in Southeast Asia. The United States joined this war. They asked the Hmong in Laos to help them. When the U.S. lost the war, Hmong people had to leave Laos.

- After 1975, many Hmong came to the U.S. as refugees. Refugees are people who escape from their country to find a new, safe place to live. Today, Minnesota is home to around 85,000 Hmong.

- Many Hmong American families enjoy outdoor activities like camping, boating, and fishing.

bitter melon—a vegetable that looks like a bumpy cucumber and tastes very bitter. It is often cooked in Hmong soups and other dishes.

bubble tea—a sweet dessert drink that comes in different flavors and has chewy black balls made of tapioca

fried bananas—bananas fried in a crunchy dough

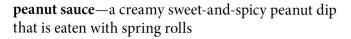

pandan—a tropical plant used as a sweet flavoring in Southeast Asian cakes and desserts

peanut sauce—a creamy sweet-and-spicy peanut dip that is eaten with spring rolls

pork and green vegetable soup—pork and leafy green vegetables boiled in a broth. This is a typical dish that Hmong families eat at mealtime.

rice in water—a bowl or plate of rice with water added to it. Many Hmong children and elderly Hmong people like to eat rice this way.

spring roll—fresh vegetables, cooked rice noodles, and meat wrapped in soft rice paper. Spring rolls are different from egg rolls because they are not fried.

GLOSSARY

audience (AW-dee-uhnss)—people who watch or listen to a play, movie, or show

auditorium (aw-dih-TOR-ee-um)—a room or building used for performances

beret (bu-RAY)—a wool or knit cap with a tight headband and a flat top

bow (BAOW)—to bend low as a sign of respect or gratitude

duet (doo-ET)—a musical piece performed by two players or singers

kennel (KEH-nul)—an enclosure with a door to keep a pet safe and contained

nervous (NER-vuss)—feeling unsure or scared

recorder (rih-KOR-dur)—a long wood or plastic musical instrument with a mouthpiece and eight finger holes

shriek (SHREEK)—to screech or scream

solo (SOH-low)—a musical piece performed by one person

spicy (SPY-see)—a strong flavor of spice that might feel hot in your mouth

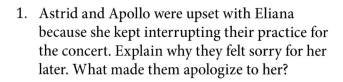

1. Astrid and Apollo were upset with Eliana because she kept interrupting their practice for the concert. Explain why they felt sorry for her later. What made them apologize to her?

2. Eliana put glue on Astrid's headband and poured milk in Apollo's shoes. Discuss the reasons why you think Eliana did this.

3. The titles of the songs for the concert were based on real songs. Can you figure out which classic songs they were based on? Talk with a friend to come up with some other silly song titles!

WRITE IT DOWN

1. At the concert, Astrid and Apollo couldn't find the sheet music for their duet. Write a paragraph to describe what you would do if you lost your sheet music right before you were about to perform.

2. Eliana made a drawing of herself in a concert with Astrid and Apollo. Be like Eliana and draw a fun picture of yourself playing any instrument you like.

3. Pretend you are the most famous recorder player in the world. Write a poem about your recorder's music and how you feel whenever you play it.

ABOUT THE AUTHOR

V.T. Bidania has been writing stories ever since she was five years old. She was born in Laos and grew up in St. Paul, Minnesota, right where Astrid and Apollo live! She has an MFA in creative writing from The New School and is a McKnight Writing Fellow. She lives outside of the Twin Cities and spends her free time reading all the books she can find, writing more stories, and playing with her family's sweet Morkie.

ABOUT THE ILLUSTRATOR

Evelt Yanait is a freelance children's digital artist from Barcelona, Spain, where she grew up drawing and reading wonderful illustrated books. After working as a journalist for an NGO for many years, she decided to focus on illustration, her true passion. She loves to learn, write, travel, and watch documentaries, discovering and capturing new lifestyles and stories whenever she can. She also does social work with children and youth, and she's currently earning a Social Education degree.